KB085279

월행

도서출판 아시아에서는 《바이링궐 에디션 한국 대표 소설》을 기획하여 한국의 우수한 문학을 주제별로 엄선해 국내외 독자들에게 소개합니다. 이 기획은 국내외 우수한 번역가들이 참여하여 원작의 품격을 최대한 살렸습니다. 문학을 통해 아시아의 정체성과 가치를 살피는 데 주력해 온 도서출판 아시아는 한국인의 삶을 넓고 깊게 이해하는 데 이 기획이 기여하기를 기대합니다.

Asia Publishers presents some of the very best modern Korean literature to readers worldwide through its new Korean literature series 〈Bilingual Edition Modern Korean Literature〉. We are proud and happy to offer it in the most authoritative translation by renowned translators of Korean literature. We hope that this series helps to build solid bridges between citizens of the world and Koreans through a rich in-depth understanding of Korea.

바이링궐 에디션 한국 대표 소설 039

Bi-lingual Edition Modern Korean Literature 039

A Journey under the Moonlight

송기원

월행

Song Ki-won

ASIA
PUBLISHERS

Contents

월행

A Journey under the Moonlight

구름 사이로 달이 빠져나오자 반짝, 개천이 드러났다. 살얼음이 낀 개천은 달빛을 받아 무슨 시체처럼 차갑게 반짝거리며 아래쪽 미루나무 숲으로 사행(蛇行)의 긴 꼬리를 감추고 있었다. 바로 그 미루나무 숲 언저리로부터 한 사내가 개천 둑에 모습을 나타내었다. 사내는 등에 누군가를 업고 있었는데, 외투로 보자기를 씌워서 멀리서 보면 흡사 곱사등 같은 모습이었다. 사내는 그런 모습으로 깊게 눌러쓴 벙거지 속의 눈빛을 세워 사방을 휘둘러보며 천천히 개천을 따라 거슬러 올라왔다. 개천의 양켠으로는 추수가 끝난 논밭들이 을씨년스럽게 버려져 있었는데, 개천의 위쪽에서 북풍이 몰릴 때

A creek flashed into view. The moon had finally fought free of the clouds and, bathed in the moon's light, the thin sheets of ice on the surface of the creek shone cold as a corpse. The long, meandering tail of the creek disappeared into the poplar-filled woods down below, and where those poplars began there appeared at the bank of the creek a man. He was carrying something on his back, but it was blanketed with an overcoat, so that from afar he looked like a hunchback. Pressed low over his face was a hat that complemented the rest of his appearance. The man looked up and glanced in all directions as he slowly followed the creek upstream. On either side of the creek lay rice paddies

마다 어디선가 마른 수수깡 흔들리는 소리가 우수수, 우수수, 빈 벌판을 울리곤 했다. 수수깡 소리가 들릴 때마다 사내는 흠칫 놀라서 걸음을 멈추곤 했다. 개천을 가로지른 신작로의 다리를 넘어서자 사내는 벙거지를 벗고 이마의 땀을 훔쳤다. 사내는 무심결에 달을 쳐다보았다. 부족하지도 넘치지도 않는 만월이 구름 사이를 빠르게 움직이고 있었다. 반백(半白)의 구레나룻으로 뒤덮인 사내의 얼굴에 어떤 음영이 서리는가 싶더니 이내 사라져버렸다. 깊은 주름살이 패고 군데군데 칼자국이 있어서 꿈틀대는 짙은 눈썹과 함께 사내의 얼굴은, 그가 막일로 평생을 살아온 사람이라는 것을 쉽게 알려주고 있었다.

문득 사내의 곱사등이 꿈틀대더니 뜻밖에 어린아이의 맑은 목소리가 흘러나왔다.

"아부지, 아직도 멀었어?"

아이의 목소리가 흘러나오자 사내의 표정이 대뜸 밝아졌다.

"아녀, 아녀. 저어기 불빛이 뵈쟈? 거겨."

사내가 손을 들어 개천의 위쪽 병풍처럼 잇닿은 연봉(連峯)들의 산자락 한켠, 몇 낱 불빛들을 가리키자,

desolate in the wake of the harvest. The occasional northerly gust whirled downstream with a rustle that announced the presence of desiccated millet stalks somewhere across the empty fields. Each hollow rustling sound startled the man, stopping him in his tracks. He crossed a bridge over the creek, removed his hat, and passed a hand across his brow. Almost as an afterthought the man looked up at the moon. It was perfectly round and full and it seemed to be speeding through the clouds. A shadow flickered across his face with its grizzled whiskers and disappeared just as quickly. Deeply defined wrinkles, knife scars, dark wriggling eyebrows—his was the face of a man who had done heavy labor all his life.

Suddenly the man's hunchback trembled and a young child's clear voice escaped from the overcoat.

"Are we there, Daddy?"

The man's face brightened at once.

"No, not yet, pumpkin. See those lights over there? That's where we're headed."

The man pointed to a few lights on the far side of the sewer creek, at the foot of a range of mountains that were joined like a folding screen.

"어디? 어디."

조막손이 사내의 낡은 외투를 헤집고, 거기에서 예닐곱 살쯤 되어 보이는 아이의 얼굴이 빠끔히 삐져나왔다.

"저기가 아부지 고향이지?"

사내는 아이의 별스럽지 않은 질문이 그러나 몹시 대견한 모양이었다. 사내는, 허허, 녀석 신통두 허지, 숫제 얼굴 가득 찬 주름살로 웃었다.

"하문. 그렇구 말구. 저기가 바로 아부지 고향이여."

사내는 따뜻한 시선으로 아이와 함께 오랫동안 마을의 불빛을 바라보았다.

개천은 마을 뒤 골짜기에서부터 시작하여 마을을 감싸고 흘러내리고 있었다. 사람들은 이 골짜기를 한실 골짜기라고 불렀고, 거기에서 시작된 개천을 한실 꼬랑이라고 불렀고, 그 마을을 한실 마을이라고 불렀다. 바로 그 한실 마을이 사내의 고향이었다. 사내의 조부의 조부 때부터 자작일촌을 이루어 내려온 마을. 큰 제사 때면 너나 할 것 없이 저마다 흰 두루마기를 내어 입고 종가댁 등불 아래 모여 신명(神明)께 축문을 드려온 마을. 제사가 끝나면 어른들은 아이들에게 자신들이 들었던 훌륭한 선친들의 이야기를 또다시 들려준 마을. 해

12

"Where? Where?"

A clawlike hand made an opening in the man's worn overcoat and the face of a boy of six or seven peeked out.

"That's your home, right, Daddy?"

The man seemed terribly proud answering this unremarkable question. *Haha—you're quite the kid.* The smile on his sincere face deepened his wrinkles even more.

"Yessir, that it is, your daddy's home, all right."

The man and the child stared with heartwarming gazes at the lights coming from the village.

From its source in the valley behind, the creek embraced the village on its downhill journey. Valley, village, and creek alike were named Hanshil. That village was the man's home. It was the village where the man's great-great-great-grandfather had established their family's farmland for generations to come, the village where everyone, all wearing their *turumagi*, gathered around the lights at the home of the village elder to perform the ancestral rites and offer the ritual prayers. It was the village where adults passed on to children, for generation after generation, the great legends that their late fathers had told them. And it was the vil-

마다 정초엔 가가호호를 돌며 한 해 액풀이를 하는 꽹과리 패들로 극성스러운 마을. 사내가 한실 마을로부터 도망친 것도 훌쩍 이십 몇 년이 넘어 버린 것이었다.

개천을 벗어나 마을 입구의 정자나무 아래 다다랐을 때, 사내는 문득 심한 기침 끝에 피를 토해냈다. 죄업이다, 라고 사내는 자조했다. 이 마을이 폐촌이 되어 버린 것처럼 자신의 병 또한 죄업이다, 라고 사내는 두 손 가득히 피를 받으며 자조했다. 허허, 사내는 벌겋게 웃으며, 우는 아이를 달래어 놓고 개천으로 내려갔다.

살얼음을 깼을 때, 사내는 수면에서 피 묻은 얼굴과 함께 달을 보았다. 달과 사내의 피 묻은 얼굴이 한데 어울려 흔들리고 있었다. 그렇게 흔들리는 자신의 얼굴을 들여다보며 사내는 어쩌면 자신의 삶도 그렇게 조악한 것만은 아니었을 거라는 생각을 했다. 물을 집어 올리려는 사내의 두 손이 떨려왔다. 달과 어울린 피 묻은 얼굴이 수면에서 울고 있었다.

마을로 들어서자 개들이 맨 처음 사내를 발견했다. 처음에 어쩌다 사내를 발견한 한 마리의 개가 으르렁거리더니 곧이어 개들의 울부짖음은 마을 전체에 퍼져서, 고즈넉하던 작은 마을은 온통 개들의 울음소리로 가득

14

lage that had grown frantic the first ten days in January, everyone running from house to house with gong in hand, chasing away the evil spirits that would remain for the rest of the year if not warded away. Some twenty years earlier—twenty years gone in a blink—the man had fled Hanshil Village.

As he came over the rise where the creek reached the shaded trees at the entrance to the village, the man coughed hard and spat a handful of blood. *This is because of my sins*, the man mocked himself. *This sickness is my punishment for turning this once lively village into a ghost town*, he said under his breath. His cupped hands pool blood. The boy began to cry. The man chuckled again, his face red now. After he had comforted the weeping child he resumed his journey along the creek.

A thin section of ice shattered and on the surface of the water the man saw his bloodstained face and the moon rippling together. As he peered down at his quivering reflection, he supposed that there might after all be some aspects of his life that were not completely dull and harsh. His hands shook as he tried to scoop water into his hands. Tears trickled down the blood-smeared face that was a part of the tableau of the moon on the water's surface.

차 버렸다.

"원, 개새끼들이라니."

사내는 가볍게 투정을 하며, 그러나 어쩐지 개들의 컹컹대는 소리도 정답게 여겨져서 혼자 미소를 띠었다. 퇴락한 초가와 낮은 토담을 지나치며 사내는 선잠이 깬 마을 사람들의 밭은기침 소리를 마치 개들의 그것처럼 여길 수 있었다. 이윽고 낯익은 집 앞에 섰을 때, 사내는 문득 자랑스러운 마음이 되어 등에 있는 아이를 토닥거렸다.

"자, 이게 아부지 집이다."

"이렇게 큰 집이 다 아부지 집이란 말이야?"

"하문, 이게 다 아부지 집이지."

"이제 우리는 여기서 살 거야?"

"하문, 여기서 살지."

"학교에도 다니고?"

"하문, 낼부텀 당장에 학교에 댕겨야제."

사내는 아이와 수작을 하며 대문을 두드렸다. 대문을 두드리며 사내는 기둥에 붙어 있는 입춘대길(立春大吉)을 보았다. 그을음이 끼고 색이 바래어 있었지만 사내는 그것이 누구의 글씨체인 줄 알 수가 있었다. 대문간

The first ones to notice the man were a pack of dogs. The dog at the front of the pack snarled at him and soon the rest were howling and barking, their cries spreading throughout the village.

"Damn dogs." But it wasn't a serious complaint, for even the baying of the dogs sounded friendly and welcoming and drew a smile from him. As he passed the low mud walls of collapsed thatched huts, he could hear the coughing of village people awakened from their slumber; their hacking affected him in the same way the barking dogs had. Presently he came to a stop in front of a familiar house and, suddenly feeling proud, he patted the boy on the back.

"Look, daddy's house, right here."

"Wow. You mean this big house is all yours?"

"You bet."

"Are we gonna be livin' here from now on?"

"Of course."

"And, I'll get to go to school?"

"Sure thing, starting tomorrow if you want."

Still chatting with the boy, he knocked on the door and, as he did so, noticed beside the door a sooty, discolored sign, a sign written in a hand he recognized: "Great Fortune in Spring." As he waited

의 어둠 속에서 사내의 얼굴이 환해져 왔다.

"살아 계셨구면. 용케도 아직꺼정 살아 계셨구면……."

사내가 소리 내어 중얼거렸다.

대문을 두드린 지 한참 만에 낯선 청년이 사내를 맞
이했다. 청년은 눈을 비비며 문간을 막아서서,

"뉘슈?"

사내에게 퉁명스럽게 말을 건네 왔다.

"여기에 이용만이란 분이 안 계시는지……."

청년은 이제 확연히 잠이 깬 눈빛으로 사내의 형색을
위아래로 살펴보며 대답을 머뭇거렸다. 사내가 다급하
게 다시 물었다.

"안 계신가?"

"제 할아버진데, 어떻게 오셨수?"

"……."

여전히 대문을 막아서서 잔뜩 의심스러운 시선으로
훑어보고 있는 청년에게 무어라고 대꾸를 해야 할지 몰
라 사내가 우물쭈물 말을 고르고 있을 때,

"태식아, 밖에 뉘라도 왔나?"

안에서 천식기 섞인 목소리가 들려왔다.

"낯선 분이 할아버님을 찾는데요?"

in the dark his face lit up.

"He's still alive," the man mumbled. "Good heaven, he's still alive..."

After a long pause the door finally opened to reveal the face of an unfamiliar young man. Blocking the entrance, he rubbed the sleep from his eyes.

"Who're you?" the young man snapped.

"Oh, I was wonderin' if a Mr. Yi Yong-man lived here..."

Now fully awake, the young man studied his visitor from top to bottom, hesitant to answer. The man asked again pressingly,

"He ain't here no more?" the man said.

"He's my grandfather—what do you want with him?" The young man continued to block the entrance, his eyes still suspicious as he surveyed the man.

The man was cautiously composing an answer when an asthmatic voice leaked out from inside. "Tae-sik, who's there?"

"Some stranger lookin' for you, Grandfather."

"Nobody with manners would be lookin' for me at this time of night."

Finally the man pushed the young man out of the way and stepped inside. Feeling his way toward the

"어허, 밤늦게 어느 분이 날 찾는단 말여."

사내는 청년을 제치고 안으로 들어섰다. 사랑채의 캄캄한 방문 앞에서 사내가 머리를 조아렸다.

"아부님 저, 저, 갑득이올습니다."

"뭬, 뭬라구?"

방문이 화들짝 열렸다.

"가, 갑득이올습니다."

"갑득이라구?"

방 안의 캄캄한 어둠으로부터 노인이 문 줄을 잡고 끄응 상반신을 밖으로 내밀었다. 허연 상투머리와 수염이 사뭇 떨리고 있었다. 그렇게 몸을 떨며 노인이 침침한 눈을 들어 달빛을 받고 서 있는 사내를 한참 동안 올려다보았다. 노인이 그르륵그르륵 가래가 끓는 목소리로 다시 물었다.

"니가 갑득이라고?"

"예, 가, 갑득이올습니다."

사내가 다시 한 번 머리를 조아리자 노인이 사내로부터 고개를 돌려버렸다.

"우리 집안엔 그런 사람 읎다."

사내가 당황하여 한 발짝 더 노인에게 가까이 다가섰다.

room from which the voice had come the man bowed deeply before the door.

"Father, it-it's me, Gap-deuk."

"Wh...What did you say?"

The door swung open to reveal an old man.

"It's Ga-Gap-deuk."

"Gap-deuk?"

With an effort the old man braced himself against the doorframe and leaned halfway out from the gloom inside. Gray topknot and beard quivering, body quaking, the old man somberly considered the erect man illuminated by the moon. In a phlegm-garbled tone he asked,

"Gap-deuk, you say?"

"Yes sir. I'm Ga-Gap-deuk."

Again the man bowed deeply, but the old man's only reaction was to turn his head away.

"Ain't nobody by that name in this family."

Bewildered, the man took a step closer.

"Fa-father."

"No. Ga-Gap-deuk died during the war."

With those words, the old man withdrew into the dark of his room. A desperate fit of coughing erupted from the old man in the room the moment he stepped inside. It sounded as though the old

"아, 아부님."

"아, 가, 갑득이는 동란 때 발, 발써 죽은 사람여."

노인은 다시 방 안의 캄캄한 어둠 속으로 몸을 숨겨 버렸다. 방 안에서 심한 기침이 쏟아져 나왔다. 금방이라도 숨이 끊길 듯이 쿨룩거리는 노인의 기침은 마치 캄캄한 방 자체가 기침이라도 하듯이 선뜻하고 요란스러웠다.

사내가 얼굴이 납빛이 되어 정신을 잃고 서 있는데, 청년이 말을 건넸다.

"저어, 큰아버님. 좀 전엔 죄송했습니다. 잠결이라 미처 알아 뵙지 못하고……. 우선 제 방으로라도 드시지요."

사내가 빛을 잃은 시선으로 청년을 물끄러미 바라보다가 중얼거리듯 입술을 달싹였다.

"니가 을득이 아들이냐?"

청년이 고개를 떨구었다.

"예."

사내는 청년으로부터 고개를 돌려 중천에 휘영청 밝은 달을 향하며 지나는 말처럼 넌지시,

"니도 날 원망하겠구먼."

얼결에 말을 받은 청년의 얼굴에 당황한 빛이 스쳤다.

man's could not possibly take another breath. The room felt chilly and clamorous as if the dark room itself had been coughing.

The man stood vacantly, his face white as a sheet.

The young man broke the silence.

"Uh, Uncle, I'm very sorry about before. I wasn't quite awake and I didn't recognize you. Please come in to my room at least."

The man stared at the young man, the brightness fading from his gaze. His lips quivered as if he were mumbling, and finally he managed to ask,

"Are you Eul-deuk's son?"

The young man dropped his head.

"Yes."

The man turned away from the young man toward the moon, bright in the middle of the sky, and when he spoke again it was as if he were addressing the moon: "You must blame me too."

This remark caught the young man off guard, and an awkward expression appeared on his face.

"Not really. It's all in the past."

The man shook his head at the young man's reply even as he continued to gaze toward the moon.

"Even if I were to meet your father in the other

"뭘요. 다 지나간 일인데요."

사내는 여전히 달에서 눈을 떼지 않은 채, 청년의 말에 고개를 좌우로 흔들었다.

"구천엘 가서도 니 애비 만날 면목이 없을껴."

청년이 힐끗 사내의 얼굴을 훔쳐보았을 때, 청년은 달빛에 음각처럼 드러난 깊은 주름살과 몇 개의 흉한 칼자국을 보았다. 그것이 이상하게도 청년의 눈에 아프게 와 박히는 것이었다. 청년은 자꾸 씀벅거리는 눈을 어쩔 수가 없었다.

"어디 그것이 큰아버님 탓이겠습니까? 다 시절이 흉했기 때문이지요."

청년이 마치 그 시절을 살아본 사람처럼 말했고, 사내는 그런 청년의 말을 못 들은 체했다.

"니 애비가 총살당하던 날 밤에 난 저쪽 골에 숨어 있었제. 물론 확성기로 떠드는 소리도 듣고 있었제. 자술허면 니 애빌 살려준다고 말여. 그래도 난 못 나갔던 겨. 결코 목숨이 아까운 것은 아녔어. 그 당시 나넌 눈깔이 뒤집혀 있었응께. 복수를 하겠다고 말여. 허허."

사내가 몸을 흔들며 침통하게 웃었다. 그러자 여태껏 잠자코 있던 아이가 사내의 등에서 칭얼대기 시작했다.

world, I wouldn't deserve to talk to him."

The young man stole a glimpse at the man's face. The deeply drawn wrinkles and the ugly scars that he saw there pained him and he couldn't help blinking.

"How is it your fault, Uncle? It's because of the times you lived in."

The young man said it as if he himself had lived during those times.

The man pretended not to have heard.

"When your father was shot I was hiding in that valley over there. I heard everything they said over the loudspeaker. They said they would spare your father's life if I turned myself in. But I couldn't. And I swear to you, it wasn't because I was afraid for my life. No, it was because I was mad for revenge..." the man laughed bitterly, his body shaking.

The boy, quiet on his father's back till then, started to whimper.

"Daddy, I'm cold. Hurry up and go inside."

The young man answered the boy before the man could.

"Gosh, where are my manners. Uncle, let's go inside. Here, give me the boy."

"아부지 추워. 추워 죽겠어. 빨리 방에 들어가."

그러자 사내보다도 먼저 청년이 아이의 말을 받았다.

"아이구, 이 정신 좀 봐. 큰아버님, 어서 방으로 들어
갑시다. 자, 우선 아이를 제게 주시고요."

"아녀, 괜찮어."

사내는 그러면서도 등에서 아이를 내렸다. 아이는 잔
뜩 웅숭그린 채 낯선 동네의 낯선 청년을 흘끔거리더니
사내에게 바싹 붙어 서서 옷자락을 잡고 놓지 않았다.
아이가 조그맣게 말했다.

"아부지 오줌 눌래, 오줌."

사내가 아이를 뒤켠으로 데려갔다.

"자, 아무 데나 누부러."

아이가 바지를 내리고 고추를 내밀자 곧이어 작은 포
물선을 그리며 오줌 줄기가 뿜어져 나와 울타리의 마른
나뭇가지들이 바스락거렸다. 아이가 사내를 돌아보았다.

"아부지, 나 오줌 세지?"

"넥키놈, 그런 소리 하는 거 아녀."

사내가 아이의 머리에 알밤을 먹였다. 그렇게 알밤을
먹이는 사내의 표정에서 이미 조금 전의 침통한 빛은
찾아볼 수가 없었다.

"Naw, it's fine." The old man let the boy down.

The boy crouched like a ball, glancing at this strange young man in this strange town and clutching at his father's leg. Softly, he said,

"Daddy, I need to pee. Pee."

The man took him to the backyard.

"Here. Go anywhere."

The boy pulled down his pants and a small arc of urine spattered against the twigs of the hedge.

"Daddy, look how strong my pee is."

"Little brat, you don't say things like that."

The man knuckled his son's head. His sorrowful expression had disappeared.

"But Daddy, I learned it from *you*," the boy murmured.

The man pulled his son's pants up and heaved a sigh. "Dear," he muttered. "How did I end up with a kid like this at my age? Hmm... Can I rest in peace leaving this young one behind?"

The man returned to the front of the house and, as requested by the young man, was removing his shoes when the old man stuck his head out from inside.

"Is Tae-sik there?"

"Yes."

"씨이, 아부지가 맨날 그래 놓고 뭐."

아이가 투덜거렸다. 아이의 바지를 추스르면서 사내의 입에서 한숨처럼 중얼거림이 새어 나왔다.

"허어, 어쩌다 늘그막에 요런 것이 생겨 가지고……. 허어, 내 이눔을 두고 곱게 눈이 감겨질지 몰라."

뒤켠에서 나온 사내가 청년의 권유대로 토방에 신발을 벗고 있을 때, 사랑채에서 노인이 다시 방 밖으로 상반신을 내밀었다.

"태식이 게 있느냐."

"예."

"뫼시고 건너오너라. 이 방도 불도 좀 밝히구……."

청년이 성냥을 켜 석유램프에 불을 댕기자 노인의 모습이 드러났다. 주름살투성이의 눈언저리에 흥건히 젖어 있는 물기를 노인은 감추지 않고 있었다. 사내가 방으로 들어서자 노인이 쯧쯧 혀를 차며 혼잣말을 했다.

"내 요즘 그렇지 않아도 죽은 메늘아기가 자꾸 꿈자리에 뵈 심사가 어지럽더니만……."

사내는 노인의 중얼거림을 귓전으로 흘려버리고, 문득 생각이 났다는 듯이 아이에게 말했다.

"민수야, 할아부지께 인살 드려야제."

"Tell them to come here and give us a bit of light."

The young man struck a match to light the oil lamp, bringing the old man's profile into sight. The old man made no effort to hide the tears at the corners of his eyes. The man entered the old man's room.

The old man tutted. "So that's why I've been seeing my dead daughter-in-law in my dreams these days," he mumbled.

The man ignored this.

"Min-su," he said to the boy. "Mind your manners and pay your respects to your grandfather."

The boy bowed low, forehead touching the floor.

"Who is this?" said the old man, gesturing with his chin toward the boy.

The man scratched his half-bald head in embarrassment.

"My son... I took a wife at a late age."

The old man nodded, taking in this information without much reaction.

"And the mother?"

"We were too far apart in years," said the man, still scratching his head. "We got acquainted in a drinking place. For a tavern girl she looked re-

아이가 방바닥에 엎드려 넙죽 절을 하자 노인이 턱으로 아이를 가리켰다.

"걘 눤가?"

사내가 겸연쩍다는 듯이 반백의 상고머리를 갈퀴손으로 긁적거렸다.

"자식 놈입니다. 늦쩨를 봤더니만 글쎄……."

노인은 알 만하다는 듯이 고개를 몇 번 주억거리더니,

"걔 에민?"

여전히 머리를 긁적거리는 사내에게 다시 물었다.

"너무 나이 차이가 졌지요. 술집에서 알게 됐는디. 작부치곤 생긴 것도 참허구, 존 일 궂은일 다 겪은 년이어서 소갈머리도 꽤 있어 뵈, 몇 년 전부터 살림이란 걸 시작했지요. 이 녀석을 난 뒤로는 그년이 꽤 살림 맛을 안 듯싶더니만 얼마 전에 어떤 젊은 놈과 정분이 났던 모양이어라우. 소문을 듣고두 모른 체 덮어 뒀는디 끝내 도망을 치구 말았수. 그래서……."

사내가 내친김에 무언가 더 할 말이 있는 듯 보였으나 노인이 팔을 휘둘러 사내를 제지했다. 노인이 청년에게 말했다.

"태식아, 손불 깨워 가지고 밤참 좀 짓도록 해라. 먼

spectable enough and she'd gone through the good and the bad and I thought she'd be responsible too. We started living together a few years ago. After the boy was born she looked like she enjoyed the home life, but then she started up an affair with some bum. I heard the rumors but I made like I didn't know about it. And then the slut ran off with him. So..."

The man seemed to have more to get off his chest but the old man gestured for him to stop.

"Tae-sik," he said to the young man. "Wake your wife up and have her fix a late snack. They've had a long journey and they must be starving."

"I'm not hungry. Don't worry about it."

"No. Tell her anyway. And then, Tae-sik, stay in your room until I call for you."

When the young man had left, the old man looked directly into the man's face. The gaze beneath the old man's swollen eyelids was surprisingly powerful.

"If it weren't for you, our family wouldn't be in this wretched state. Do you know how many men in our family were killed after you took off?"

The soot stain on the lamp threw a flickering shadow on the old man's face. The wrinkles in the

길 오느라고 허기졌을 텐디."

"밥 생각 없어라우. 그만두도록 허슈."

"아니다. 짓도록 해라. 그리고 태식이 넌 내 부를 때까지 니 방에 가 있거라."

청년이 나가자 노인이 정면으로 사내를 바라보았다. 짓무른 눈꺼풀 속에서 뜻밖에 형형한 눈빛이 나타났다.

"니놈만 아니었어도 우리 집안은 이토록 망하지는 안 했을 것이여. 니놈이 도망간 후로도 니놈 대신에 집안 장정들이 몇이나 죽어 나간 줄 아냐?"

램프의 그을음이 그림자가 되어 노인의 얼굴 위에서 어른거리고 있었다. 그림자 속에서 주름살들이 실룩거렸다.

"뻔뻔도 하제. 무슨 염치로 다시 이 땅을 밟을 생각이 났단 말이냐."

방 안은 잠시 침묵이 감돌았다. 그들이 무거운 침묵에 가슴을 짓눌리고 있을 때, 아이가 가볍게 코를 골기 시작했다. 추위에 떨다가 몸이 녹자 졸음에 겨웠던 모양으로, 아이는 어느새 사내 곁에서 새우잠을 자고 있었다. 노인의 시선이 아이의 얼굴에 가 닿고, 그렇게 한참 동안 아이의 자는 양을 보고 있더니,

shadow were twitching.

"You've got a lot of nerve. Aren't you ashamed to set foot on this land again?"

Silence hung heavy in the room, deadening their hearts. The silence was broken by the faint snoring of the boy. Once he'd stopped shivering and his body had warmed up, sleep had taken over him and before anyone knew it the boy was curled up in a ball beside his father. The old man's gaze turned to the boy's face and remained there awhile.

"He looks just like his father. Here, lay him out comfortably." The man moved away from the sleeping mat so the boy could stretch out there. The man carried the boy to the vacant spot, settled him there, and covered him with a blanket.

With his hand resting on the boy, the man spoke again.

"I know this ain't a place I should have set foot in again, but I just feel so sorry for this young'un... Father, I don't think I have much time left in this world."

The old man burst out angrily, "You're tellin' me that after all the people you butchered and ate, you won't be livin' a long life?"

For the first time the man felt a need to explain

"애빌 빼닮았구먼. 일루 펜하게 눕혀라."

자신이 깔고 있던 요의 한 귀를 비켜주었다. 사내가 아이를 안아 눕히고 이불을 덮어주었다. 사내가 아이에게서 손을 떼지 않은 채 말했다.

"못 올 덴지 알지만 어린것이 너무 불쌍해서……. 아부님, 전 아무래도 오래 못 갈 것 같습니다."

사내의 말에 노인이 벌컥 역정을 냈다.

"그렇게 많은 목숨을 잡아묵고도 오래 못 살어."

그러자 사내가 처음으로 자신의 일을 변명했다.

"미쳤지요. 지가 미쳤지요. 세상에 지 여편네가 그런 꼴을 당하고도 안 미칠 놈 있답디여."

사내의 눈에 핏발이 서는 듯했다. 노인도 지지 않았다.

"그런 꼴을 당한 놈이 어디 니놈 혼자뿐이었다냐. 피했으면 되는 거여. 눈 꾹 감고 피해 살았으면 되는 거여. 우리 조상님들은 다 그렇게 이 마을을 지켜온 거여."

노인과 사내가 격양해서 다투고 있을 때 방문 밖에서 젊은 아낙네의 목소리가 들려왔다.

"할아버님, 진짓상 차렸는디요."

"들여보내라."

젊은 아낙네가 밥상을 들여왔다. 노인이 말했다.

himself.

"I was crazy. I was out of my mind, I tell you. I mean, is there any fellow who wouldn't go mad after seeing his wife go through all that?"

The man's eyes looked bloodshot. But he didn't back down.

"You think you're the only man who's ever suffered through that? Instead, you could have avoided it. All you had to do was shut your eyes, avoid it, and go about your business. That's how our beloved ancestors protected our village."

In the midst of their heated argument, a woman's voice seeped in through the door to the room.

"Grandfather, the food is ready."

"Bring it in."

In came a young woman carrying a portable meal table.

"Eat," said the old man. "When you're done, there's somewhere you and I have to go."

The man looked over at the old man, who proceeded to tidy up his attire with an air of perfect nonchalance. He retied his messy hair into a topknot, put on his hat, and donned a white *turumagi*. The man made a pretense of being finished and pushed away the meal tray. The old man got up.

"묵어라. 묵구 나서 나허구 갈 데가 있다."

"……?"

사내가 노인을 건너다보자 노인은 아랑곳없이 의관을 챙겼다. 흐트러진 머리칼을 모아 다시 상투를 꼽고, 갓을 쓰고, 흰 두루마기를 입었다. 사내가 시늉만으로 상을 물렸다. 노인이 먼저 일어섰다.

"자, 가보자."

노인과 사내가 방문을 나서자 청년이 놀란 눈으로 그들을 지켜보고 있었다.

"아니 이 밤중에 어디를 가시려고 이러십니까?"

"이 밤 안으로 꼭 해야 할 일이 있어."

"그렇다면 저도 따라가겠습니다."

노인이 손을 저어 청년을 물리쳤다.

"일없다. 넌 따라올 곳이 못 돼."

그들은 한실 골짜기로 접어들었다. 인기척에 놀란 밤새들이 푸드득, 숲 사이를 날아다녔다. 골짜기가 깊어짐에 따라 달빛도 스며들지 않았다. 둘은 길을 더듬으며 자칫 넘어지곤 했다. 사내가 말했다.

"지가 앞장서지라우."

사내는 노인이 한실 골짜기로 접어들 때부터 어렴풋

"All right, let's go."

Outside, the room the young man greeted them with a look of surprise.

"Wait, where are you going at this late hour?"

"There's something that must be done before the night ends."

"In that case, I'm coming with you."

The old man flicked his wrist in a gesture of dismissal.

"Don't need you. It ain't a place for you."

The two men entered Hanshil Valley. Startled birds, sensing humans approaching, scattered through the woods, their wings fluttering. They walked deeper into the forest, until the moonlight no longer penetrated it. As they groped their way along, they stumbled from time to time.

"I'll go first," the man said. All along he had been vaguely speculating where they might be headed.

The old man readily gave way.

They reached a ridge, by which time both men were hacking continually.

"Let's rest a bit," the old man called out. He sat down and spat out some mucus.

The man sat down at a distance and coughed up a wad of mucus with blood tinged in it. He made

이 행선지를 짐작하고 있었다. 노인이 선선히 사내에게 자리를 비켜주었다. 골짜기를 타고 올라 산등성이에 이르렀을 때에는 둘 다 그르륵그르륵, 가래를 끓이고 있었다. 노인이 사내를 불렀다.

"쉬었다 가자."

노인이 먼저 자리를 잡고 앉아 끓는 가래를 뱉어 내었다. 사내 역시 노인에게서 떨어져 앉아 피 섞인 가래를 뱉어 내었다. 노인이 사내를 힐끗거렸다.

"무슨 병이냐?"

사내는 구태여 숨기지 않았다.

"폐병인 모양이우."

노인이 물끄러미 사내를 건너다보며 가래 섞인 목소리로 말했다.

"내 눈에 흙이 들어가기 전에 니놈을 이곳으로 끌고 오다니, 신명께서 도우셨다. 이젠 죽어도 여한이 없다."

사내가 일어서서 골짜기 아래를 눈으로 더듬었다. 골짜기에서부터 부챗살처럼 펼쳐 나간 벌판에는 가득히 달빛이 내려앉고 있었다. 달빛, 달빛뿐이었다. 그 달빛에 사내는 어쩐지 눈이 시렸다. 사내는 마른 눈을 비비고 또 비비며 달빛을 내려다보았다. 그러자 달빛 속에

no effort to hide it.

The old man glanced at the small wet pool of blood and saliva in the man's hand. "What's the matter?"

"I think it's my lungs."

The old man fixed him with a stare. "You bastard," he stammered, "I never thought I'd be bringing you to this place while I was still alive. Now, thank God, I can die and I won't hold no grudge."

The man rose and took in the valley below. The moonlight shone full on the fields that spread out like a folding fan. Moonlight... Moonlight was everywhere. And somehow it felt cold in his eyes. Staring at the moonlight below, he rubbed his dry eyes over and over. And then in the moonlight he noticed a group of people, each in a white *turumagi*, walking along somewhere. Someone was striking a gong; the ringing, rippling, and pulsing into his ears. It would be good to be buried here and now, it occurred to him.

"All right, let's go."

This time the old man led the way. They followed the slope to where the trees ended. Above was bare rock. A sudden gust of wind buffeted them.

The old man clutched his *turumagi* and surveyed

서 흰 두루마기를 입은 사람들이 어디론가 몰려가고 있었다. 사내의 귀에 가득히 꽹과리 소리가 밀물져 들어왔다. 사내는 바로 사내가 선 자리에 뼈를 묻히고 싶다고 생각했다.

"자, 그만 가보자."

노인이 이번엔 앞장을 섰다. 등성이의 가르맛길을 타고 오르자 산 중턱쯤에서부터 숲이 끊기고 벌거벗은 민둥산이 나타났다. 갑자기 산바람이 세차게 몰아쳐서 그들을 허우적거리게 했다.

노인이 두루마기 자락을 움켜잡고 바람 속에 서서 민둥산을 훑어보았다.

"버렸어. 산두 그때 다 버렸어. 포탄으루 맥이란 맥은 다 끊어버리구……. 다아 니눔들 때문이여."

사내도 노인의 시선을 따라 민둥산의 곳곳에 움푹움푹 패어 있는 포탄 자국들을 보았다. 새삼스럽게 사내의 귀에는 쾅쾅 터져 나던 포탄 소리가 들리는 듯했다. 사내가 마치 그것들을 털어버리려는 듯 머리를 흔들며 빨리 말했다.

"가지라우."

민둥산을 가로질러 다음 골짜기에 이르자 기울기가

the bare rock.

"It was all ruined, the mountain and everything else. The bombs destroyed any spirits that ever existed here... You and the others like you, it's your fault too."

The man followed the old man's gaze to the craters where the bombs had exploded on the bare rock. Suddenly the man was shaking his head, as if the explosions were ringing in his ears at that very moment.

"Please lead the way," he managed to say.

Across the bare rock was a valley where the land was more or less level. The old man stopped at this point.

"Here." He turned back to the man. "The only place where the bombs didn't hit."

Burial mounds were scattered among the evergreens on the level ground. The man turned away from the mounds, a frightened look on his face.

"You need to apologize. All these lost souls. Dead because of you."

The man hesitated, lacking the words to reply.

"What are you waiting for?" the old man barked. "Hurry up and start your apologies. You need to beg their forgiveness."

비교적 완만한 평지가 나왔다. 노인이 멈추어 섰다.

"여기여."

노인이 사내를 돌아보았다.

"그래도 맥이 다치지 않은 데라군 이 산에서 여기뿐여."

사내는 평지의 진솔 사이 여기저기 흩어져 있는 봉분들을 보았다. 사내가 얼굴에 두려운 기색을 떠올리며 봉분들에서 눈을 돌렸다.

"사죄해라. 이게 다 니놈 때문에 생기신 원혼들이여."

"……."

사내가 머뭇거리자 노인이 날카로운 음성으로 재촉했다.

"아, 뭘 해? 빨리 엎드려 잘못을 빌지 않구."

사내가 가까운 봉분 앞에서 이 배를 올리고 무릎을 꿇자, 노인이 뒤에서 떨리는 음성으로 말했다.

"그게 을득이여."

사내는 노인의 떨리는 음성을 듣는 순간, 가슴속 저 밑바닥에서부터 무언가 뜨거운 것들이 차오르는 것을 느꼈다. 회오도, 분노도, 슬픔도 아닌 어떤 형언키 어려운 것들이 저 골짜기 아래 가득한 만공(滿空)의 달빛처럼 사내를 부풀리는 것이었다. 사내의 얼굴에서 굵은

The man knelt before the nearest grave, preparing to bow.

"That's Eul-deuk," the old man quavered.

Hearing the old man's trembling voice, the man felt something hot rising from the bottom of his heart. Not remorse, hate, or sorrow, but something difficult to express. It welled up within him like the fullness of the moonlight. A thick teardrop fell from his eye onto a blade of grass. He moved from mound to mound, and as he knelt at each to extend a long overdue apology, the old man stood behind him, telling him that this was Uncle's second child, this was his elder cousin's grandchild, this was so-and-so, introducing each lost soul. With each introduction a face appeared in the man's head for a split second.

When he arrived at the very last mound, the men knelt after bowing twice.

The old man turned away.

"That's... your wife."

The man lifted his eyes up at the mound. In his mind he could see the corpse of his wife. She was flat on her back, stark naked, a dagger stuck in her groin. Because she had their first baby her stomach had looked unusually bloated. The man felt pow-

눈물이 떨어져 내려 마른 풀잎을 적셨다. 사내가 하나 하나 봉분을 옮겨 가며 무릎을 꿇을 때마다 노인은 뒤에서, 그게 당숙 둘째 자제여, 그게 사촌 형님 손자여, 그게 뉘여, 사내에게 일일이 소개를 했고, 그럴 때마다 사내는 잠깐씩 얼굴들을 떠올렸다.

맨 끝에 있는 봉분에 이르러 사내가 이 배를 하고 무릎을 꿇었을 때, 노인이 사내에게서 고개를 돌렸다.

"그건…… 니놈의 처여."

사내가 눈을 들어 봉분을 바라보았다. 문득 사내의 시선에 아내의 시체가 비쳐왔다. 발가벗은 채, 사타구니 사이에 단도를 꽂고 나자빠진 모습이었다. 만혼의 아내가 처음 가졌던 아랫배 부분이 유난히 불러 보였었다. 사내의 입술을 뚫고 기어코 흐느낌이 새어 나왔다. 봉분을 옮길 때마다 가슴 저 밑바닥에서부터 비롯하여 차츰 차오르던 어떤 것들이 급기야 거센 분류가 되어 밖으로 터져 나오는 것이었다. 사내는 두 손으로 아내의 시체를 파며 울었다. 노인이 길게 탄식을 했다.

"허어, 아무리 인종이 막돼먹은 세상이라지만……."

낫으로 뒤통수를 찍으면서도 사내는 아내의 시체를 떠올렸었고, 공사판에서 함마를 휘두르면서도, 도살을

erless as his lips parted and he began to sob, the feelings rising from the bottom of his heart, building with every mound he had visited, finally gushing forth in a violent cascade. The man wailed as he dug up his wife's corpse.

The old man heaved a deep sigh.

"Hell, for all the misbegotten people in this world, still..."

It was always his wife's dead body that the man had thought about. When he jabbed the back of that man's head with a sickle, when he threw the hammer at the official announcement board, when he was working as a butcher, when he was looking for that runaway bitch, when he gulped down shot after shot of cheap *soju*, he was always picturing his dead wife.

The man was showing no sign of rising but the old man urged him on: "What's the holdup? Get a move on already."

"You mean there's more?" the man sobbed to his father.

"There's more."

The old man led the way to a mound far off from the others.

Here too the man was about to bow, when he

하면서도, 도망친 계집년을 찾으면서도, 막소주를 들이
켜면서도 사내는 아내의 시체를 떠올렸었다.

사내가 일어설 기미를 보이지 않자 노인이 재촉을 했다.

"뭘 꾸물거리는겨. 빨리 일어서지 못허구."

사내가 울음이 멎지 않은 음성으로 노인에게 말을 건
넸다.

"또, 또…… 있단 말이우?"

"있다."

노인은 다른 봉분들과는 달리 외따로 떨어져 있는, 그
래서 사내가 미처 알아보지 못했던 한 봉분으로 사내를
데려갔다. 사내가 봉분 앞에서 엎드리려 하자, 노인이
만류했다.

"그건 사죄헐 필요 읎다."

"……?"

"그건 니놈이여."

"……예?"

노인이 차가운 시선으로 힐끗 사내를 쳐다보았다.

"아, 우린 죄다 니놈을 죽은 사람으로 치부했으닝께.
설사 니놈이 살아 있는 걸 알았다손 치더라두 어떻게
니놈두 없이 다른 원혼들을 묻는단 말이여?"

felt a hand holding him back.

"No need to apologize to that one."

The man looked puzzled.

"That's you."

"Me?"

"You," said the old man with a cold stare. "You were as good as dead to us. Sure, we figured you were alive somewhere, but those lost souls wouldn't rest in peace unless you were buried too."

A trace of indignation rose on the man's face, and the old man looked away.

"Your name's no longer in the family register. We reported you dead—we couldn't stand the thought of you alive..."

The man coughed violently. He continued to cough increasingly violently. And just when it sounded as though he had coughed up all the mucus inside him, he coughed up a handful of blood.

The old man tore off a section of his *turumagi*.

"Here, use this."

Without a word the man took the scrap of cloth and cleaned the blood from his face and hands, rubbing red into the white of the fabric. And with this image came another image of the moon and his blood-stained face floating in harmony on the

노인을 바라보는 사내의 표정에 일순 애매한 표정이 스치자 노인이 사내의 표정을 피했다.

　"니놈은 호적에도 읎다. 사망신고를 했어. 살어남은 사람은 살어야 허닝께……."

　사내가 갑자기 기침을 하기 시작했다. 쿨룩, 쿨룩, 쿠루욱…… 온몸의 가래를 훑어 올리는 듯한 심한 기침 끝에 사내는 한 움큼의 피를 토해냈다. 노인이 부욱, 두루마기 자락을 찢어 사내에게 내밀었다.

　"닦어라."

　사내는 잠자코 두루마기 자락을 받아 얼굴과 손의 피를 씻었다. 흰 두루마기 자락에 핏빛이 선명하게 묻어났다. 문득 사내의 두 눈에 달과 함께 수면에서 흔들리던 피 묻은 얼굴이 어른거렸다. 사내가 말했다.

　"아부님, 전 인제 아무 데도 못 가겠수."

　노인이 강하게 고개를 저었다.

　"안 된다. 니놈은 이 마을에서 살지 못할 놈여."

　"아무래도 죽을 목숨이우."

　"죽드라도 타처에 가서 죽어라."

　"아부님."

　사내가 노인 앞에 엎드렸다. 노인이 백랍 같은 표정으

surface of the water.

"Father, I can't go on."

The old man gave a resolute shake of his head.

"You must. You are not welcome in this village."

"I'm going to die soon anyway."

"Then do it somewhere else."

"But Father."

The man suddenly prostrated himself before the old man, as if pleading with him. The old man rose, pushing him away with an icy coldness, and said, "Get out of here now. I'll take care of your boy."

At the village entrance under the poplar-filled woods the moon was visible suspended above the serrated crest of the mountains. For the last time the man bowed to the old man.

"Then, Father, I'll..." The man couldn't finish.

The old man flicked his wrist.

"All right. Go."

The man turned and began to stagger away.

When the man was almost out of sight the old man called out to him, "Let me know before you die and I'll settle your affairs for you."

Before long the old man's view of Gap-deuk grew blurred, and then he could no longer see him. He was still standing there when he toppled

로 그런 사내를 떼치고 일어섰다.

"이 길루 곧장 떠나가라. 자식 놈은 내가 맡으마."

노인과 사내가 마을 입구 정자나무 아래 다다랐을 때에는 달이 톱날 같은 연봉에 걸려 있었다. 사내가 노인을 향해 허리를 굽혔다.

"아부지 그럼……."

사내가 말끝을 맺지 못하고 머뭇거렸다. 노인이 손을 저었다.

"어서 가."

사내가 몸을 돌려 비칠비칠 걷기 시작했다. 저만큼 멀어질 즈음에 노인이 사내의 등을 향해 외쳤다.

"죽게 되믄 연락해라. 내 니놈 뒷수습은 해줄 테닝께."

이윽고 노인은 앞이 침침해지면서 사내의 모습이 보이지 않았다. 노인이 선 자리에서 나무토막처럼 푹 쓰러졌다.

달이 졌다.

「아름다운 얼굴」, 문이당, 2006

over like a felled tree.

The moon went down.

Translated by Jane Lee

해설

Afterword

해원(解寃)과 복원(復原)

석형락 (문학평론가)

여로(旅路)의 서사구조를 지닌 소설들이 있다. 이런 소설에서 인물에게 여행은 익숙한 곳에서 낯선 곳으로의 모험을 의미하며, 인물은 여행의 과정에서 타인을 만나거나 사건을 겪으면서 내적으로 변화한다. 물론 길을 나선 나그네가 돌아올 때, 그를 따뜻하게 맞아줄 고향은 이미 전제되어 있다. 어쩌면 모든 나그네는 돌아오기 위해 길을 나서는 것일지도 모른다. 그런데 여기서 우리가 살펴볼 송기원의 단편「월행」은 '고향→타향→고향'의 여로가 전도된, '타향→고향→타향'의 서사구조를 보여준다. 20여 년간 고향을 떠나 있던 사내(갑득)가 만월이 비추는 밤에 고향을 찾아오지만 결국 다시

Appeasing Angry Spirits and Restoring Community

Seok Hyeong-rak (literary critic)

In many novels, we can see the writer has adopted the traditional journey narrative structure. The journey is an adventure from a familiar place to an unfamiliar one. The character experiences an inner transformation through this journey by encountering strangers or events. Of course, this wanderer can always assume that he will be to return safely home, welcomed with open arms. Perhaps, this is why all wanderers leave in the first place; they leave in order to return.

In Song Ki-won's "A Journey under the Moonlight," however, this traditional narrative structure is reversed. Instead of the usual progression of "home→

고향을 떠나게 된다는 것이 소설의 골격이다. 「월행」이 우리에게 보여주는 이러한 전도된 서사구조에서 인물은 새로운 모험을 찾아 길을 나선 자가 아니라 고향으로부터 추방된 자이며, 그가 돌아온 고향은 여행에 지친 그를 맞아줄 평화롭고 안락한 공간이 아니라 이미 파괴되고 죽어버린 공간이다. 그렇다면 어째서 「월행」은 이러한 서사구조를 지닐 수밖에 없는가. 바로 여기에 한국현대사가 겪어온 고통과 시련의 과정이 자리 잡고 있다.

1945년 8월 한국은 일제의 강제점령으로부터 해방된다. 하지만 곧이어 북위 38도선을 경계로 북쪽은 소련군에 의해, 남쪽은 미군에 의해 분할 점령된다. 각자의 단독정부를 수립한 남한과 북한은 서로의 체제를 부정하고 대립했으며, 이런 대립이 내전의 양상으로 폭발한 것이 1950년 6월에 발발한 한국전쟁이다. 3년간 진행된 이 전쟁으로 한국은 대규모의 인적, 물적 피해를 입게 되고, 이전부터 내려오던 다수의 문화적 전통이 단절되고 만다. 「월행」은 한국전쟁 당시의 참혹한 실상과 공동체의 붕괴, 전통의 단절을 전라남도의 한 마을에서 대대로 살아온 일가족의 비극을 통해 압축적으로 보여준

away→home," this story progresses "away→home →away." A character (Gap-deuk) returns home under the moonlight after twenty years of wanderings only to leave again. In the reversed "A Journey under the Moonlight" the character has not left home in search for an adventure, but has been expelled from his hometown. His hometown is not a space for a peace and comfort; it is a space of utter decimation. So, why does "A Journey under the Moonlight" utilize this reversed journey structure? The reasons for this have to do with the painful and trying history of modern Korea.

Korea was liberated from a brutal Japanese occupation in the August of 1945. However, the division of the country and the occupation of the North by the Soviet Union and the South by the U.S. immediately followed on the heels of this liberation. South and North Korea established separate governments, both rejecting the legitimacy of the other. They were pitted against each other, and this confrontation exploded in the civil war now commonly known as the Korean War. During this three-year war, Korea suffered enormous human and material losses, simultaneously losing many aspects of its age-old cultural traditions in the pro-

다.「월행」의 배경인 전라남도에서, 당시 북한군과 이에 동조하는 세력은 지리산을 중심으로 거점을 잡고 있었다. 이들은 밤을 틈타 인근 마을에 내려와 식량을 조달했고, 우익적 성향의 사람들을 포섭하거나 살해했다. 날이 밝아지면 국군과 경찰이 마을을 돌며 빨치산과 내통한다는 혐의를 씌워 마을 사람들을 살해했다. 이 과정에서 이데올로기적 대립과 상관없는 다수의 부녀자와 아이, 노인들이 목숨을 잃었다.「월행」에는 갑득의 아내가 "발가벗긴 채, 사타구니 사이에 단도를 꽂고 나자빠진 모습"이 나오는데, 이러한 충격적인 장면은 우리에게 당시의 참상을 환기시킨다. 아내의 처참한 죽음에 분노한 갑득은 자수 권고를 거부하고, 그 대가로 그의 아우를 비롯한 친지들이 처참하게 살해당한다.

그렇다면 한국전쟁이 일어나기 전 갑득의 고향은 어떤 공간이었는가.「월행」에서, 갑득의 고향은 "조부의 조부 때부터 자작일촌을 이루어 내려온" 농촌이다. "큰제사 때면" 가족과 친지들이 모여 조상께 축문을 드리고, "어른들은 아이들에게 자신들이 들었던 훌륭한 선친들의 이야기를" 들려준다. "정초엔 가가호호를 돌며 한 해 액풀이를 하는" 평화로운 마을이다.「월행」이 우

cess.

"A Journey under the Moonlight" depicts the miserable conditions of these wartime conditions in sparse and unflinching detail, paying particular attention to the collapse of communities and the disruption of traditions through the tragedy of a single multi-generational village family. "Moonlight," begins in Jeollanam-do where North Korean troops and North Korean sympathizers hold strongholds in nearby Mt. Jiri and its surrounding areas. During the night, they procure their food by raiding nearby villages and winning over or killing right-leaning citizens. By day, South Korean troops and police forces patrol these same villages, killing villagers suspected of colluding with communist guerrillas. Throughout this ordeal, hundreds of innocent civilians lose their lives including—in a gruesome scene—Gap-deuk's wife, who is described as lying "flat on her back, stark naked, a dagger stuck in her groin." Perhaps more than some of the other deaths described in "Moonlight," this death in particular evokes this inescapable nightmarish bind that period's wartime conditions. Seemingly somewhat cognizant of this himself, Gap-deuk refuses to turn himself in and sets off a vicious chain of

리에게 보여주는 이러한 묘사는 한국에서 일반적으로 볼 수 있는 농촌 공동체의 풍경이기도 하다. 지역마다 조금씩의 차이가 있기는 하지만, 대체로 한국의 농촌 공동체는 한 해가 시작되는 정월 초사흘 경부터 대보름 사이 집집마다 돌아다니면서 액막이굿을 한다. 굿이 시작되면 마을의 각 가정에서는 술과 음식을 마련하여 서로 나눠먹는다. 이러한 의례는 제의적인 의미가 강한 행사이면서, 동시에 마을 축제로 기능하는 놀이문화가 되기도 한다. 액운(厄運)을 막고 풍년(豊年)을 기원하는 굿은 마을 구성원들의 공동체 의식을 고취하고 구성원들을 통합하는 기능을 수행한다. 그런 의미에서 마을 사람들은 단순히 한 마을에 같이 사는 사람들이 아니라 공통된 믿음과 공동의 문화를 공유하고 있는 사람들이다. 또한 제사는 전통적인 한국의 가부장 사회에서 중요하게 생각하는 의례 중 하나로서, 조상과 자손을 이어주는 기능을 수행한다. 집안에 큰 제사가 있으면, 평소에 떨어져 있던 가족과 친지들이 모두 모여 조상의 은덕에 감사드린다. 이들은 흰 두루마기 옷을 갖춰 입고 조상에 대한 예를 차린 후 축문을 올린다. 집안의 어른들은 나이 어린 아이들에게 조상의 삶에 대한 이야기

events, eventually resulting in the grisly murder of his relatives including his younger brother. So, then, what kind of place was Gap-deuk's hometown before the Korean War? According to "A Journey under the Moonlight," it was a farming village "where the man's great-great-great-grandfather had established their family's farmland for generations to come." During "ancestral rites," family members and relatives gathered to recite ritual prayers, and "adults passed on to children, for generation after generation, the great legends that their late fathers had told them." It was a peaceful village where everyone ran "from house to house... chasing away the evil spirits that would remain for the rest of the year if not warded away."

These brief descriptions in "A Journey under the Moonlight" are fairly typical of actual Korean farming village scenery of the time. Although there were some variations according to the region, Korean agricultural communities in general did perform shamanistic ritual from house to house on the first fortnight of the year to ward off evil spirits. When the ritual began, every family in the village prepared wine and food to share amongst each other. This shamanistic ritual was also a festival, a

를 구술로 전달한다. 그러나 한국전쟁 당시 일가족이 모두 또는 거의 죽임을 당하는 경우가 많아, 제사 및 가족사 구술 등의 문화가 대부분 파괴되고 만다. 특히 15세 이상 45세 미만의 젊은 남성들이 다수 사망함으로써, 가족과 마을 공동체에서 전승되던 전통문화를 계승할 주체가 거의 사라져 버린다. 여기에 더해 전쟁 당시 억울하게 죽임을 당한 사람들이 많아, 살아남은 사람들에게 죽은 사람들의 원혼을 달래는 해원과 붕괴된 가족 및 공동체의 복원이 큰 과제로 남게 되었고, 이들은 이 과제를 마무리해야만 새로운 삶을 모색할 수 있었다.

이처럼 「월행」은 단순히 전쟁과 이데올로기 대립으로 인한 한 사내의 비극적 삶을 보여주는 것에 그치지 않고, 전쟁 이후 살아남은 모든 한국인들의 암담한 상황과 앞으로의 과제를 압축적으로 보여준다. 해원이 이뤄지지 못한 갑득의 고향은 그가 떠나 있는 동안 시간이 정지된 상태로 멈춰 있었다. 고향을 찾은 갑득은 아버지가 살아 있음을 알고 기뻐하지만, 사실 갑득의 아버지 용만은 죽고 싶어도 죽을 수가 없었던 것이다. 용만이 갑득으로 하여금 죽은 아내와 친지들의 묘 앞에서 치르게 한 속죄 의식은 억울하게 죽은 사람들의 원한을

part of village recreational culture. At the same time, this ritual of chasing away evil spirits and praying for a year of abundance played a pivotal role in enhancing community spirit and consolidating the roles of village members. In this sense, villagers were not simply people cohabitating in the same village, but were actively and continually sharing common beliefs and culture. Additionally, ancestral rites were performed year-round and were events of foremost importance in maintaining a patriarchal society, connecting ancestors and descendants from generations and generations back. During large ancestral rites, all family members and relatives, including those away from home, gathered together to thank their ancestors for the benefits they bestowed upon them. Fitted with traditional white coats, they performed these rites and recited ritual prayers. In this way, adults would pass on to their children the legends handed down to them.

But this culture of passing down ancestral rites and oral family history telling were mostly destroyed during the Korean War with entire, or almost entire families being routinely wiped out. Also, because a significant portion of young men

풀기 위해서뿐만 아니라 살아남은 사람들이 새로운 삶을 향해 나아가기 위해서 반드시 거쳐야 하는 해원 행위이다. 그러니 아들을 떠나보내고 용만이 쓰러진 것은 바로 해원의 마무리와 태식과 민수로 대표되는 새로운 세대의 삶의 가능성을 시사한다. 하지만 「월행」이 죽은 사람들에 대한 해원과 파괴된 공동체의 복원을 전적으로 희망적이게 그리고 있는 것은 아니다. 용만이 갑득을 끝내 받아들이지 못한 것은 고향이 아직도 그를 받아들일 만한 환경이 되지 못했음을 의미한다. 용만이 폐병으로 인해 얼마 남지 않은 삶을 고향에서 보내기 위해 찾아온 아들을 다시 내쫓은 것은 그 얼마 남지 않은 삶이나마 지켜주고 싶었기 때문이다. 작가 송기원이 「월행」을 통해 말하고 싶었던 것은 '죽임'의 폭력 속에서도 포기할 수 없는 '살림'의 인간성이 아니었을까. 정전 60주년을 맞은 지금도 한국은 당시 억울하게 학살당한 모든 사람들의 명예 회복과 위령제라는 제도적 장치의 마련에 힘쓰고 있다. 그런 의미에서 「월행」이 우리에게 제기하는 해원과 복원의 과제는 아직도 현재진행형이다.

between the age of fifteen and forty-five died, the subjects who would succeed their predecessors as receptacles of traditional culture would disappear, forever interrupting the transmission of information from families and villages. Additionally, there were a huge number of other innocent victims unjustly killed throughout the war. Survivors were, then, left with the task of restoring families and communities by appeasing angry spirits. It was impossible for them to move on and search for a new life before they fulfilled this task.

Thus, "A Journey under the Moonlight" is not simply the tragic story of a man caught between the two sides of war and ideology; it is a concise picture of the dire outlook and arduous tasks survivors of the Korean War had to face. Without appeasing the ireful spirits, Gap-deuk's hometown remains in the past, frozen in time. Returning home, Gap-deuk is happy to find his father alive. But his father, Yong-man, is alive simply because he cannot die, even if he wanted to. The ritual of atonement Yong-man has Gap-deuk perform in front of his wife's and other relatives' graves is an act of appeasing bitter spirits, a necessary act not only to leave innocent victims in peace, but also for future survivors to move forward with their lives. Therefore, Yong-man's collapse after sending off his son suggests the possibility of a new life for a new generation represented by Tae-sik and Min-su.

Still, this short story's vision for the future is not entirely bright. Yong-man's ultimate rejection of Gap-deuk signifies that his hometown is not entirely ready to accept him. With his son suffering from consumption, Yong-man sends him away although his son has returned to his hometown in order to spend his last moments there. Nevertheless, Yong-man sends him away to protect his son's last moments alive. Perhaps, then, Song wishes to examine the ultimate humanity of "saving life," something that can never be given up in the midst of however much bloodshed. Sixty years after the Korean War armistice, we are still trying to arrange improved institutional solutions to restore the honor of victims. In that sense, the tasks of appeasing angry spirits and restoring communities have not ended.

비평의 목소리

Critical Acclaim

구름 사이로 달이 나오자 살얼음 낀 개천이 차갑게 반짝이며 드러난다. 그 개천의 아래쪽 미루나무 숲 언저리로부터 텁수룩한 차림의 한 사내가 등에 누군가를 업고 개천 둑에 모습을 나타낸다. 송기원 씨의 단편「월행」은 이렇게 시작하여 그 사내가 몸을 비칠거리며 마을에서 떠나는 것으로 끝난다. 작가는 원고지 60장 정도의 짧은 분량 속에 한 사내의 불행한 인생뿐만 아니라 민족사의 가장 침통했던 한 과거를 고도의 예술적 형상력(形象力)에 의해 압축하고 있다. 이 작품은 단편소설의 정석적(定石的) 기법에 따라 단일한 사건을 단일한 인물에 의해 단일한 효과에 흡수되도록 최대의 절제

"The moon had finally fought free of the clouds and, bathed in the moon's light, the thin sheets of ice on the surface of the creek shone cold as a corpse. The long, meandering tail of the creek disappeared into the poplar-filled woods down below, and where those poplars began there appeared at the bank of the creek a man. He was carrying something on his back..." Song Ki-won's "A Journey under the Moonlight" begins in this way and ends with the man staggering away from his village. The author offers us not only the tragic story of a man but also elegantly presents the darkest parts of our history in a story of less than

를 하고 있다. 그러나 그 정석적 구성에도 불구하고 어떤 틀에 얽매였다는 느낌을 조금도 주지 않으며 첫 장면이 불러일으킨 호기심과 긴장으로부터 마지막 장면에 이르기까지 잠시도 독자를 놓아주지 않는다. 아마도 송 씨의 이「월행」은 우리 단편문학사에 길이 남을 수작일 것이며, 그 치열한 작가정신에 의해서뿐 아니라 미학적 완성도에 의해서도 우리 문단의 상업주의와 안일성에 대한 심각한 경종이 될 것이다.

염무웅

단편「월행」「집단」들과 요즘의 그의 정광(精鑛)과 같은 소설들은 잔인하리만큼 정직하며 참다우며 소주 빛깔의 투명한 저항의 능력을 갖추고 있다. 따라서 그의 작가의식이라는 것, 작가의 현실의식이라는 것에 있어서도 매우 단속적으로 발전하고 있다.

고은

「월행」은 그 출발이었다. 이 작품은 어디 한 군데 틈이 보이지 않도록 쩽쩽하다. 작가의 눈은 달빛이 되어 20년을 떠돌다 어린 자식을 안고 귀향하는 죽음을 앞둔

4,000 words. "Moonlight" exercises a high degree of restraint and self-control, following the classical formula for a short story where a single event by a single character results in a single effect. Despite this restraint, however, Song's story flows naturally, maintaining the reader's interest from beginning to end. Song Ki-won's "A Journey under the Moonlight" is an outstanding work of art that will forever be remembered in the annals of Korean short stories. It is also a somber warning against the commercialism and laziness in our literary world, warning us through both its solemn authorial spirit and its aesthetic perfectionism.

Yeom Mu-ung

Like shards of purified ore, Song's recent short stories—such as "A Journey under the Moonlight" and "Group"—are brutally honest and powerfully transparent like the clearest of *soju*. In this way, Song's authorial awareness and attitude towards reality have also progressed consistently.

Ko Eon

"A Journey under the Moonlight" was the beginning. This story is so tightly woven that no gaps are

사내와 어린 손주만 거두고 자식을 떼미는 노인의 비통한 심경을 감싼다. 노인과 사내가 어느 달밤에 연출하는 이 기막힌 드라마는 작가가 시「친화(親和)」에서 노래한 바로 그 세계이기도 하다.

미미한 것들은 미미한 것들끼리 알몸을 껴안는다.
숨어 사는 친구여, 눈을 뜨고 바라보라.
멍든 안개들은 멍든 안개들끼리 서로의 멍을 애무하고
달빛은 긴 붕대처럼 내려 그 멍을 감싼다.
횡포한 자의 눈에는 보여지지 않고 드러나지 않는다.

「월행」이 아내와 아우가 살해된 6·25의 비극적 현장으로 한 사내가 귀향하는 이야기라는 점을 주목하기 바란다. 그것은 바로 횡포한 자의 눈에는 가리어진 민중사의 진실로 작가 송기원이 귀의하는 것이기도 하기 때문이다.

최원식

「월행」은 한 폭의 은은한 느낌을 주는 동양화 같은 작품이다. 달빛이 비추면서부터 시작되어 달이 짐과 동시

visible in it anywhere. The author's eye becomes the moonlight and embraces the sorrows of a man who has returned home with a young son after twenty years of wandering, and an old man who takes in only his grandson and while pushing his own son away. This awe-inspiring drama produced by an old man and his son under the moonlight is also about a world Song once sang about in his poem, "Affinity."

Trifling ones embrace each other's naked bodies.

My friend in hiding! Open your eyes and look at them!

Bruised fogs caress each other's bruises,

Moonlight, coming down like a long bandage, wraps around those bruises.

Violent ones cannot see them; they are invisible to their eyes.

"A Journey under the Moonlight" is a story of a man who returns home to a tragic site of the Korean War, a village where his wife and younger brother were brutally murdered. This is also Song Ki-won's return to the truth of our history invisible to the eyes of those who perpetrated it. Choe Won-sik

에 끝을 맺는 이 작품은 시종일관하여 흐르는 '부족하지도 넘치지도 않는 만월' 속에서 펼쳐지는 비극적인 사건을 담담하게 기술하고 있다. 6·25 동란 중 아내와 아우를 살해당한(어느 쪽에 의해 살해되었는지는 작품 속에서 제시되어 있지 않다) 한 사내가 그 일로 인해 20여 년을 떠돌다가 마침내 병들어 고향을 찾아가지만 결국 안주하지 못하고 다시 떠나야 하는 비장한 이야기를 작가는 지극히 객관적인 어조로 서술하고 있다.

현준만

"A Journey under the Moonlight" is like a subtly crafted Oriental painting. This story begins with the appearance of moonlight and ends with the setting moon, serenely describing a tragic event that evolves under a full moon... With a kind of cold objectivity, Song narrates a tragic story in which a man returns home ill after twenty years of wandering because of a tragic wartime incident, the murder of his wife and brother (it's not clarified which side killed them).

Hyeon Jun-man

송기원

송기원은 1947년 음력 7월 1일 전라남도 보성군 조성
면에서 태어났다. 단편 「월행」의 배경이 조성면에 있는
한실마을이다. 방장산과 존제산으로 둘러싸인 이곳은
빨치산의 주된 근거지였던 지리산으로 이어지는 탓에
한국전쟁 당시 이념 대립으로 인한 피해가 극심했던 곳
중에 하나이다. 생부인 송만섭은 장터의 건달로 노름과
아편에 빠져 있었고, 이를 견디지 못한 생모 최홍임은
해산물 중간상인인 이천우와 새 가정을 꾸렸다. 어린
시절 송기원은 해산물을 파는 어머니를 따라 장돌뱅이
로 성장했다. 그는 '사생아'와 '장돌뱅이'라는 조건을 통
해 자신이 사회적으로 천대받는 위치에 있음을 인식했
고, 이런 인식은 그의 소설에서 '자기혐오' 또는 '자기부
정'으로 나타났다. 그는 자전적 소설이나 에세이들에서
자신이 '더러운 피'를 가졌다는 자격지심에 시달렸다고
말한 바 있다. 1963년 광주에 있는 조선대학교 부속고
등학교에 진학하지만 곧 낙향하고, 짧은 기간 장터 건
달들의 똘마니 노릇을 하기도 한다. 이 시기 그는 사회

Song Ki-won

Song Ki-won was born in Joseong-myeon, Boseong-gun, Jeollanam-do on the first day of the seventh lunar month in 1947. Hansil village in Joseong-myeon is the background of his short story, "A Journey under the Moonlight." As Hansil village was surrounded by Mt. Bangjang and Mt. Jonje, branched from Mt. Jiri, a guerrilla stronghold during the Korean War, it suffered severe consequences during the war in the midst of the country's ideological conflicts.

Song's birth father, Song Man-seop, was an inveterate gambler and alcoholic. As a result, Song's mother, Choe Hong-im, remarried Yi Cheon-u, a seafood merchant. Song Ki-won grew up as a peddler's son, following his new family around from fair to fair. As a stepchild and a peddler's son, Song was acutely aware of his low social status. As a result, this awareness was embodied in his novels' and stories' main characters' self-abhorrence and self-negation. In his autobiographical works, he frequently noted that he suffered from feelings

나 자신에 대하여 반항하는 종류의 책들을 닥치는 대로 읽어치운다. 1966년 고려대학교 주최 전국 고교생 백일장 대회에서 시「꽃밭」을 투고하여 당선되고, 이것이 계기가 되어 그는 암담하기만 한 자신의 삶에 일말의 가능성이 있음을 깨닫게 된다. 1967년 고등학교 3학년 때 전남일보 신춘문예에 시「불면의 밤에」를 투고하여 당선되고, 이듬해 서라벌예술대학(이후 중앙대와 통합됨) 문예창작과에 입학한다. 1969년 동아일보 신춘문예에 시「후반기의 노래」를 투고하여 가작으로 입선한다. 같은 해 5월에 입대하고, 이듬해에 월남전에 참가하지만 말라리아에 걸려 귀국한다. 1974년 동아일보 신춘문예에 시「회복기의 노래」가, 중앙일보 신춘문예에 단편「경외성서(經外聖書)」가 당선되어 문단에 나온다. 1972년 12월 대통령 박정희가 장기 집권과 독재를 위해 국민의 기본권을 침해하는 유신헌법을 공포하자, 1973년 학생과 시민들이 헌법개정 청원운동으로 이에 맞서고, 1974년 1월 문인들이 헌법개정 청원운동 지지선언을 하게 된다. 이에 국군보안사령부가 지지선언에 서명한 문학평론가 임헌영, 소설가 이호철 등을 간첩으로 몰아 처벌하는데, 이것이 문인간첩단 사건이다. 서라벌예술대

of self-condemnation for his "dirty" blood.

Song's career path to literary star was a steady, but somewhat troubled one. Although he entered Chosun University High School in Gwangju in 1963, he took a leave of absence and returned home where he briefly worked as a henchman at fairs. He was an avid reader of books that dealt with social and personal issues during this period. Shortly afterwards, he won an award at the nationwide high school student writing contest held by Korea University in 1966 with his poem, "A Flower Garden." This brief moment of accolades seemed to give him hope for his future in writing. Indeed, in just one year later he won the *Jeonnam Ilbo* spring literary contest award as a high school senior with his poem, "On a Sleepless Night." His literary path continued then when he entered the department of creative writing at Seorabeol Arts College (later merged with Chung-ang University) the next year. In 1969, his poem, "Song of the Second Half" won the merit award at the *Dong-A Ilbo* spring literature contest. His literary career was briefly interrupted then when he was drafted in May the same year and dispatched to Vietnam the next. However, shortly after his dispatch he contracted malaria and

학에서 이호철의 강의를 들은 바 있는 송기원은 이 사건에 크게 분노한다. 같은 해 7월 반독재 투쟁의 상징인 시인 김지하가 국가보안법 위반과 내란선동죄로 사형을 선고받자, 11월 시인 고은, 소설가 이문구, 황석영 등의 문인들이 '자유실천문인협의회'를 결성하고, '문학인 101인 선언'을 하게 된다. 이들은 선언문에서 '자유민주주의의 정신과 절차에 따른 새로운 헌법의 마련' '구속 시인의 석방' '언론·출판·집회·결사의 자유 보장' 등을 주장한다. 당시 문단 신인인 송기원도 이 선언에 함께 참여하게 되는데, 이 사건을 계기로 그는 이전의 탐미주의적인 경향을 탈피하고 역사의식에 눈을 뜨게 된다. 1977년 문예지 《창작과비평》에 단편 「월행」을 발표하고, 1979년 창작집 『월행』과 장편 『해 뜨는 집』을 출간한다. 1980년 그는 '김대중 내란음모 사건'에 연루되어 투옥된다. 박정희가 암살된 후 정권을 잡은 신군부가 당시 유력한 야당 정치인인 김대중을 간첩으로 몰고, 그가 계획한 민주화추진 국민운동계획에 내란음모라는 누명을 씌운 일이 '김대중 내란음모 사건'이다. 당시 중앙대 복학생이었던 송기원은 '유신잔당 상여 데모'를 하다가 이 사건에 연루된다. 당시 신문은 그가 '김대중으

was sent home. He made his full literary debut in 1974, when he won top honors at the *Dong-A Ilbo* spring literary contest with his poem "Song of Convalescence," and the *Joongang Ilbo* spring literary contest with his short story, "Apocrypha."

Like many writers of the time, Song eventually became deeply involved in the country's turbulent political affairs. When President Park Chung-Hee declared the Yushin Constitution to extend his dictatorship indefinitely in December 1972, students and citizens resisted Park's actions with the Constitution Amendment Petition movement in 1973. Subsequently, a large number of writers joined as well, crafting with a formal declaration in support of the Constitution Amendment Petition movement in January 1974. In response, Military Security Headquarters arrested writers en masse including critic Im Heon-yeong and writer Yi Ho-chol, arresting them on the grounds of spying for North Korea for which the military fabricated a Writer-Spy Cell Incident to bolster their claims.

An attendee of Yi Ho-chol's lectures in college, Song was irate regarding this incident. When in July of that same year the poet Kim Ji-ha, a symbol of anti-dictatorship resistance, was sentenced to cap-

로부터 문교부의 간부 자리를 약속받고 '내란음모에 가담한 일당'이라고 썼다. 이 사건으로 그는 12년형을 선고받고 수감되는데, 아들이 간첩으로 몰린 것을 한스럽게 여긴 어머니가 수감된 아들과의 면회를 거부당하자 스스로 목숨을 끊고 만다. 1982년 12월에 형집행정지로 출소한 뒤, 이듬해 시집『그대 언 살이 터져 시가 빛날 때』를 출간한다. 그는 이 시집으로 제2회 신동엽 창작기금을 받는다. 1984년 창작집『다시 월문리(月門里)에서』를 출간한다. 월문리는 경기도 화성군에 있는 농촌으로, 그는 1978년 무렵 어머니와 함께 월문리로 이주했다. 송기원은 월문리에 살면서 농촌의 경제와 구조에 관심을 가지게 되었고, 국가독점자본주의 아래에서 농촌이 어떻게 수탈당해왔으며, 농민들은 어떻게 대응하는가에 대해서 깨닫게 되었다고 말한 바 있다. 1985년 실천문학사 주간으로 일하면서, '『민중교육』지 필화사건'에 연루되어 투옥되었다가, 이듬해 석방된다.『민중교육』지는 실천문학사에서 내는 비정기 간행물로서 주로 한국의 교육 현실을 정치적, 이데올로기적 시각으로 분석한 논문을 실었다. 문교부는『민중교육』지에 실린 논문들이 '반미감정 선동' '계급의식 고취와 자본주의체

ital punishment, writers Ko Eon, Yi Mun-gu, and Hwang Sok-yong formed the Writer's Association for the Practice of Freedom and declared the "101 Writers Declaration" in November. In this declaration they demanded "a new constitution according to the spirit and procedure of liberal democracy," "the release of detained poets," and "the guarantee for the freedom of press, publication, assembly, and association."

Song's participation in this movement became a turning point in his literary and personal life. He left his aestheticism behind and turned to a new mode of writing that emphasized historical consciousness. His short story "A Journey under the Moonlight" was published in the literary quarterly *Changbi* in 1977 and, in 1979, a collection of short stories of the same title and a novel entitled *The House of Rising Sun* were published to great acclaim. In 1980, Song was imprisoned in connection with the Kim Dae-jung Rebellion Conspiracy Incident, an incident that had been fabricated by the new military junta that had taken power after the assassination of Park Chung-hee. After he was sentenced to a twelve-year term, his mother committed suicide after frustrated attempts at visiting him to prison.

제 부정' 등의 내용을 담고 있다는 보도자료를 배포하고, 결국 실천문학사 주간인 송기원, 교사 윤재철과 김진경이 국가보안법 위반혐의로 구속된다. 송기원은 이듬해 6월 석방된다. 1990년 그는 실천문학사에서 펴낸 오봉옥 시인의 시집『붉은 산 검은 피』가 반공법에 걸려 시인과 함께 투옥된다. 같은 해 시집『마음속 붉은 꽃잎』을 출간하고, 1993년 단편「아름다운 얼굴」로 제24회 동인문학상을 수상한다. 이후 장편『너에게 가마 나에게 오라』(1994), 창작집『인도로 간 예수』(1995), 장편『여자에 관한 명상』(1996), 장편『청산』(1997), 장편『안으로의 여행』(1999), 장편『또 하나의 나』(2000)를 출간한다. 2001년 단편「폰개성」으로 제9회 오영수문학상을 수상한다. 2003년 창작집『사람의 향기』를 출간하고, 이 창작집으로 제11회 대산문학상, 제6회 동리문학상을 수상한다. 이전의 소설이 체험을 바탕으로 하여 '자기혐오'나 '자기부정'을 형상화했음에 비할 때, 『사람의 향기』는 타인의 목소리를 들으려 하고 그들의 상처 많은 삶을 긍정하고 있다고 평가받는다. 2006년 시집『단 한번 보지 못한 내 꽃들』을, 2011년 소설 형식의 도덕경(道德經) 해설서인『못난이 노자』를 출간한다. 현재는 안성에

After he was released in December 1982 when the execution of his term was suspended, his poetry collection, *When the Poetry Shines through the Crack of your Frozen Skin*, was published the next year. This book brought him the Shin Dong-yeop Creative Writing Fund.

In 1984, his short story collection, *In Weolmun-ri, Again*, was published. Weolmun-ri was a farming village in Gyeonggi-do that he had moved to with his mother around 1978. Song mentioned that he had become interested in agriculture and its economic structure here and had learned how state monopoly capitalism exploited farmers as well as how farmers had responded to it. In 1985, when he was working as editor-in-chief of Silcheon-munhak Publisher, he was imprisoned again in relation to the *Minjung Education* Incident. He was released in June next year. The Ministry of Education distributed press release in which it accused *Minjung Education*, education journal published by Silcheon-munhak, of "anti-American sentiment provocation" and "encouragement of class consciousness and negation of capitalist system." He was imprisoned again together with poet O Bong-ok in 1990, for violating the Anti-Communism Law, with O's poet-

있는 작업실에서 글을 쓰고 있다.

ry collection, *Red Mountain Black Blood*. The same year, his poetry collection, *Red Petals in My Heart*, came out, and in 1993, he won the 24th Dongin Literary Award for his short story, "Beautiful Face."

His published works in the following years include the novel, *I'll Go to You, Come to Me* (1994), the short story collection *Jesus Gone to India* (1995), and the novels, *Reflections on Women* (1996), *Blue Mountains* (1997), *Journey Inward* (1999), and *Another Me* (2000). He won the 9th Oh Yeong-su Literary Award in 2001 for his short story, "Pongaeseong," in 2001. In 2003, he won the 11th Daesan Literary Award and the 6th Dongri Literary Award in 2003 with his short story collection, *Scent of a Human*. Since then, more of his work have been published to great critical acclaim including the poetry collection, *My Flowers I Could Not See Even Once* (2006), and a book of commentaries on *Tao Te Ching* written as a novel, *Laozi, a Simpleton*. Song is currently writing full-time at his studio in Seong-geo in Anseong.

번역 **제인 리** Translated by Jane Lee

제인 리는 브리티시컬럼비아대학교의 브루스 풀턴 교수와 함께 한국 단편 소설 번역 강의에서 송기원의 『월행』을 번역했다. 2009년에 브리티시컬럼비아대학교에서 무역학 학사학위를 받았다.

Jane Lee translated Song Ki-won's *A Journey under the Moonlight* (Wal-Heng) in a Korean short story translation class with Professor Bruce Fulton at the University of British Columbia. She graduated with a Bachelor's in Commerce from UBC in 2009.

감수 **전승희, 데이비드 윌리엄 홍**
Edited by Jeon Seung-hee and David William Hong

전승희는 서울대학교와 하버드대학교에서 영문학과 비교문학으로 박사 학위를 받았으며, 현재 하버드대학교 한국학 연구소의 연구원으로 재직하며 아시아 문예 계간지 《ASIA》 편집위원으로 활동 중이다. 현대 한국문학 및 세계문학을 다룬 논문을 다수 발표했으며, 바흐친의 『장편소설과 민중언어』, 제인 오스틴의 『오만과 편견』 등을 공역했다. 1988년 한국여성연구소의 창립과 《여성과 사회》의 창간에 참여했고, 2002년부터 보스턴 지역 피학대 여성을 위한 단체인 '트랜지션하우스' 운영에 참여해 왔다. 2006년 하버드대학교 한국학 연구소에서 '한국 현대사와 기억'을 주제로 한 워크숍을 주관했다.

Jeon Seung-hee is a member of the Editorial Board of ASIA, is a Fellow at the Korea Institute, Harvard University. She received a Ph.D. in English Literature from Seoul National University and a Ph.D. in Comparative Literature from Harvard University. She has presented and published numerous papers on modern Korean and world literature. She is also a co-translator of Mikhail Bakhtin's *Novel and the People's Culture* and Jane Austen's *Pride and Prejudice*. She is a founding member of the Korean Women's Studies Institute and of the biannual Women's Studies' journal *Women and Society* (1988), and she has been working at 'Transition House,' the first and oldest shelter for battered women in New England. She organized a workshop entitled "The Politics of Memory in Modern Korea" at the Korea Institute, Harvard University, in 2006. She also served as an advising committee member for the Asia-Africa Literature Festival in 2007 and for the POSCO Asian Literature Forum in 2008.

데이비드 윌리엄 홍은 미국 일리노이주 시카고에서 태어났다. 일리노이대학교에서 영문학을, 뉴욕대학교에서 영어교육을 공부했다. 지난 2년간 서울에 거주하면서 처음으로 한국인과 아시아계 미국인 문학에 깊이 몰두할 기회를 가졌다. 현재 뉴욕에서 거주하며 강의와 저술 활동을 한다.

David William Hong was born in 1986 in Chicago, Illinois. He studied English Literature at the University of Illinois and English Education at New York University. For the past two years, he lived in Seoul, South Korea, where he was able to immerse himself in Korean and Asian-American literature for the first time. Currently, he lives in New York City, teaching and writing.

바이링궐 에디션 한국 대표 소설 039
월행

2013년 10월 18일 초판 1쇄 인쇄 | 2013년 10월 25일 초판 1쇄 발행

지은이 송기원 | **옮긴이** 제인 리 | **펴낸이** 방재석
감수 전승희, 데이비드 윌리엄 홍 | **기획** 정은경, 전성태, 이경재
편집 정수인, 이은혜 | **관리** 박신영 | **디자인** 이춘희
펴낸곳 아시아 | **출판등록** 2006년 1월 31일 제319-2006-4호
주소 서울특별시 동작구 흑석동 100-16
전화 02.821.5055 | **팩스** 02.821.5057 | **홈페이지** www.bookasia.org
ISBN 978-89-94006-94-9 (set) | 978-89-94006-02-4 (04810)
값은 뒤표지에 있습니다.

Bi-lingual Edition Modern Korean Literature 039
A Journey under the Moonlight

Written by Song Ki-won | **Translated by** Jane Lee
Published by Asia Publishers | 100-16 Heukseok-dong, Dongjak-gu, Seoul, Korea
Homepage Address www.bookasia.org | **Tel.** (822).821.5055 | **Fax.** (822).821.5057
First published in Korea by Asia Publishers 2013
ISBN 978-89-94006-94-9 (set) | 978-89-94006-02-4 (04810)